MARCIA TUCKER THREE STORIES

EDITED BY MARION BOULTON STROUD

DESIGNED BY TAKAAKI MATSUMOTO, MATSUMOTO INCORPORATED

PUBLISHED BY ACADIA SUMMER ARTS PROGRAM

Published by Acadia Summer Arts Program

Marion Bolton Stroud, Publisher
Takaaki Matsumoto, Matsumoto Incorporated, New York, Producer and Designer
Amy Wilkins, Manager of Publications

Printed and bound by Nissha Printing Co., Ltd., Kyoto, Japan

Cover photograph: Taylor Castle, *Untitled*, 2005

Library of Congress Control Number: 2008900883
ISBN-13: 978-0-9797642-1-9

Distributed worldwide by D.A.P./Distributed Art Publishers
155 Sixth Avenue, 2nd Floor
New York, New York 10013
Tel: (212) 627.1999
Fax: (212) 627.9484
dap@dapinc.com
www.artbook.com

I HEAR YOU

The day Ed was supposed to go for his final fitting, he had a fight with his son about the trip he'd been planning for the two of them. He'd been on the phone with the boy, giving him some pointers on how to use a .22-gauge. Aim a little low, he told him, because the gun will jerk up until you get used to the action of the rifle and you can coordinate your breathing with the trigger pull. He'd gotten Keith the gun for his fifteenth birthday a few weeks back—not that he'd asked for it, but it was time. A boy should learn to shoot when he's young enough for it to become second nature.

Fanny had never liked Ed's hunting, wouldn't eat anything he brought back. It had to do with all that reading she did. She'd gotten it into her head that killing anything was wrong. What did she think, meat comes all cut and pre-packaged, like in the supermarket? That the slaughterhouse is a better way for an animal to die than a nice clean shot to the neck when the thing doesn't know what's coming? She hadn't wanted him to keep his guns in the house, even though the cabinet was locked. Well, what she wanted didn't matter any more.

Keith hadn't seemed all that interested in the .22.

"Thanks, Dad," he'd mumbled when he unwrapped the package. Ed had included all the hunting gear he'd need as well. "Wait till the other guys get a load of this. It's cool. They'll be jealous for sure." But Keith's face had a kind of flat look, almost like he was asleep, and his eyes skittered off to one side. Not like when Fanny got him a Scrabble set a few years back. He had thrown his arms around her, laughing, insisting that she sit down and play with him right away.

Come to think of it, the boy never seemed to look directly at Ed any more. Maybe it was his age. Teenage boys shuffle around a lot, stare at the ground, smack each other on the back, talk in monosyllables. Had he been that way too? He didn't think so. Ed liked to look a guy square in the eye when he was talking, stay with him. It made a good first impression. It's a salesman's best tool. Once in a while it makes the other guy uncomfortable, and when he looks away you know you're going to clinch the deal, get the price you want. Look a guy straight in the eye, and you know who's running the show.

Like hunting. When you shoot, you'd better have your eye on the target. You learn that. Even when the animal looks at you like it knows it's about to die and you're the one who's going to make that happen, you've got to face it head on. That's honest hunting. Bagging a deer was okay—good for making venison stew once in a while—but it was turkeys he really loved to go after. When it came to turkey hunting, he was one of the best callers around. He could mimic the one-to eight-note hoots of a barred owl with his voice—the sound that got the hens all excited. It was a lot harder than using a locating device to flush them out, although he was really good at those, too. Hardly anyone could use the mouth calls as well as he could. He'd hunt turkeys any time he could, starting early in the season and ending late, after he was sure that there was no chance of finding any strays.

Ed pictured the two of them, him and his boy, out in the woods side by side. He'd teach Keith how to do a slate call, to work a pair of push-peg calls simultaneously to mimic fighting toms, to pattern his purrs till the hens called back. It's kind of like talking. When you hear the yelps and clucks, you know the jakes are looking for the nest. But it's the gobbles you're going for. What you want is a tom, one of the big fellas.

Keith would have fun once he got the hang of it. It would be great. He'd give his kid what he himself always wanted, the thing his own father was too busy for—time together. Maybe he'd even give the kid a nip from the flask, just to show him that Ed could be a pal too, not just a father. Ed's own father had never asked him a single question, not that he could remember, anyways. "Pass the potatoes." "Do your homework." "Get the firewood." "Feed the dog." Ed could almost feel Keith's skinny body as he put his arms around his shoulders from behind, showing him how to hold the .22 properly, supporting him till he got used to the recoil. He imagined the two of them walking back through the woods at dusk, tired and happy, silently lugging their bagged birds.

They had been pals not so long ago. He remembered the warmth of the boy's cheek as he bent to kiss him goodnight, the small arms reaching up to wrap themselves around Ed's neck. "Night-night, sonny-boy," he'd say, "sleep tight, don't let the bedbugs . . ."

"Bite!" Keith would cry, and snuggle into the covers as Ed ruffled his hair gently, then eased himself out the door, leaving it ajar in case the kid woke up scared.

In the past year or so Ed had mostly hunted deer. Although no one could come close to his turkey calls, a lot of the time he missed the bird's response, or couldn't quite make out where it was coming from. Unless the damn things were right on top of him, the hens yelping, he tended to come back empty-handed. His own father had been a little deaf, but Ed thought it was because of the logging, the noise of the saws and the trees crashing. He didn't think you could inherit it, although he'd been noticing lately that most people mumbled, that he was saying "What?" a lot. It wasn't serious enough for him to do anything about it. It was hunting, though, that finally got him to make an appointment to have it checked out.

Now he wasn't even sure he needed the damned contraption. If he and Keith were going to be hunting together regularly, he could count on the boy's young ears to track where the sounds were coming from and how far away they were, how fast they were moving. Ed figured Keith would feel useful, proud of being able to help his father.

The argument started when he told Keith that he was taking him out to the woods on Saturday, that he wanted him to be up and ready by 4:00 a.m. The kid seemed to sleep sixteen hours out of twenty-four, always rolled up in the funky sleeping bag he kept open on the top of the mattress, big feet hanging off the edge of the bed. The room smelled of socks and something else, like mayonnaise gone bad. It was supposed to be Ed's study, but he'd put a single bed and dresser in there so Keith could stay over weekends, or whenever Fanny, who had custody, would agree to it. Which wasn't all that often, not any more. Ed had gotten his own place after they broke up, a temporary apartment in town till they got back together, he thought. But it had been two years already; and he was beginning to think that maybe it wasn't going to happen.

Ed had been looking forward to the trip. When he thought about him and Keith going out to the woods together, he got this feeling like he used to have just before the county fair opened. The days just before slowed way down, and he'd be itchy with waiting. He'd have saved up for weeks, not spending a penny of what he earned stocking shelves for his mother down at the store, planning and plotting what rides he'd go on, what games he'd try, what treats he'd buy for himself. He wanted to make the most of his time, and this was no different. Keith would spend the weekend with him, so there was no chance he'd oversleep. He'd talked to Fanny about it three or four times, even after they'd agreed on the days and the time, just to make sure.

His hand on the receiver was sweaty. "I've worked it out with your mother," Ed said. "Come over after school on Friday, bring your camo and boots, and don't forget the cap I got you. Your goggles too. And gloves, don't forget your hunting gloves."

Keith didn't answer, but Ed figured maybe he was writing it all down. "I was thinking," Ed added, "we'd try going out to Black Hawk Ridge." It was the best turkey hunting spot in Wisconsin. Maybe in the whole Midwest. "Not many people up there, because it's a tough climb. I've been scouting it for a couple weeks now, and it looks good."

Suddenly there was a rush of sound in the receiver. Keith was talking, but Ed didn't understand what he was saying. "I'll pack us up a lunch," Ed went on, "and I'll start you out with a few of the simple calls, till you get the hang of it." Keith said something else. The boy was trying to get a word in, but damn it, Ed wasn't finished with what he was saying. Kids were always interrupting their parents, and he wasn't going to let his son get away with it. "I can't go, Dad," Keith said loudly. "I have a date."

It took a moment for Ed to get the gist of it. "What did you just say?" he asked.

"I have a date," Keith repeated.

"Well, that's just too damn bad," Ed said. "This is the one weekend that works for me and for your mother both. She told me she has to go out of town to visit her sister. I've been working on this trip a long time."

There was silence on the line. Then a cough. "Dad, I don't want to," Keith said. His voice was whiny. "It's a school dance, and I can't just tell Sally that I'm not going to take her now. It's too late. I don't want to."

Ed's teeth ground against each other. "There's no discussion, son," he said. "I'll see you on Friday."

"No, you won't!" Keith yelled. "I'm not going, and you can't make me. I don't want to go hunting with you. I hate hunting. And you can take your stupid gun back, too. I don't want it, I never wanted it in the first place."

The boy's voice caught, and Ed could hear him begin to cry. If there was anything he hated, it was tears. Especially in a boy. Ed had never cried, not once, even when he broke his arm when he was learning how to ride a bike.

"What kind of sissy are you, anyhow?" he growled.

Keith slammed the phone down.

Ed thought of Barton's son, about the same age. Gus was big, like his dad, and even when he was a tyke he was always begging his father to take him fishing, hunting, climbing. Anything that Barton did, Gus wanted to do too.

He wished that Fanny would move somewhere else, to the other side of the country, to Alaska. And take Keith with her. He wished they'd both drop dead. He didn't want to think about them, either of them, any more.

Ed and Fanny had been high school sweethearts. She wasn't one of the popular girls, but she had her own friends and always had lots to do. She was a little on the chubby side, not so much that you'd remark on it, but she was no cheerleader type, either. She had long dark hair cut off straight at the bottom, small round eyes, and a dimple in her chin. When she laughed, which was most of the time, you could see a gold tooth twinkling back there, just inside the edge of her bright red mouth. She liked to wear tights and those kind of loose shirts with round collars. Most girls Fanny's size didn't wear tights because they showed too much of a good thing, but not Fanny. She didn't give a shit what anyone thought, as long as she was comfortable. She liked the way she looked, and he guessed he did too, because he was always trailing after her, hoping she'd stop and say hello. Soon enough, she did.

Ed was quiet, but she didn't seem to mind, because she was always so bubbly, so interested in everyone else, busy planning things, sewing her own clothes, working on projects, getting people together. He loved the way she moved, the energy she had.

"Eddie," she'd say, running up to him at school, breathless, "you'll never guess what happened!" And she'd launch into a rapid-fire recital, sentences tumbling over one another, punctuated with giggles. Matt had come in late and got a detention, and you know what that means, because he's had two already. She'd seen Sue and Jimmy holding hands in the stairwell, and wasn't that just the cutest thing—they were made for each other. She was going to be at drama club after school, but if he wanted to he could come by and see a little of the play, she'd love to know what he thought of it, and maybe he could give her a hand with the set, she wanted to try the sofa and table in a different place, but she'd have to do it when Miss Gravek wasn't there.

Fanny did her homework on time, didn't care much about television, not like most of the kids. She was always trying to convince him to read some book or other, even though she knew he wasn't particularly interested.

What he did best was to be there for her. Anything she wanted, he would do. He had always had been good at fixing things. He fixed things around her house, like the broken window in her room, the dresser drawer that had gotten stuck, or the ceiling fan that had stopped working. Her parents, who both worked, thought it was great that Ed wanted to help out and had the time to do it.

He repaired Fanny's bike, filled the tires with air, put a bell on the handlebar, got a basket and rack for it so she could carry stuff. Whenever she talked, he listened as though her voice was the only sound in the world. No one had ever been interested in him before. When he saw her in the hall, looking around for him, he felt a feeling flood his chest like the sun was shining from the inside. This was what it felt like to be happy. It was an excited, skittery feeling, one that teetered on the edge of being something bad but at the last minute turned around. It was like being on a roller coaster, the relief you feel when you find yourself slowly going back up the track after you've just been scared shitless going down.

Junior year he asked her to wear his ring and she agreed. Maybe she liked him because he was the strong, silent type, or because he didn't get in her way. He wasn't bad looking, medium height, five foot eleven, with straw-colored hair that he wore long, with sideburns. He could never figure out what it really was that appealed to her, just that he was one lucky dude. He could hardly believe it when she finally decided to go all the way with him. She hadn't done it before, she said, but she was ready. She loved him.

There was a whole lot he wanted to tell her, but he never seemed to get around to it. Ed wasn't used to talking to people. Maybe because he was an only child, so he'd spent a lot of time on his own. When his father came home from logging camp, which wasn't all that often, it would be peaceful for a day or two, the three of them having dinner together and his parents sleeping late in the morning, but then it would change. Sooner or later his mother would be standing on the sagging porch, cigarette in one hand, B & B in the other, her mouth open, screaming at his father's retreating back. Ed tried to stay out of her way, which wasn't all that hard because she spent most of the time in her room, off in her own world. It was his father he had to watch out for, because if his dad didn't stalk off into the woods after one of their fights, he'd come looking for Ed. It was best to disappear.

One morning, after a lot of shouting and crying and plates breaking in the kitchen, his father stalked into the woods. Ed left for school. When he got home, he found his mother, gray-faced, strands of dyed red hair falling in her face, pacing back and forth in the living room, chain-smoking. She didn't look at Ed. When he asked her what was going on, she didn't answer. Instead, she grabbed her jacket and peeled off in the pickup, and when she came back she had the Sheriff and another man, wearing a suit, with her.

"The minute I heard that shot," his mother said to the men, her back to Ed, "I knew."

Less than a week after the funeral she disappeared, leaving Ed a rubber-banded wad of bills with a note around it. In her cramped handwriting, it said how sorry she was, how she didn't have any choice, she couldn't take it any more, how he was old enough now to take care of himself and even though she knew it was wrong, there it was. She told him to remember to feed the dog. He had just turned sixteen.

She never came back, and Ed never tried to find her, either. He didn't say anything about her leaving, just went on as always, and no one seemed to notice that he was on his own. He did odd jobs after school, pumping gas, delivering groceries, mowing lawns or shoveling snow, depending on the season.

So there was no one around to tell him what he should or shouldn't do, about Fanny or anything else. Her parents felt sorry for him, and when he and Fanny announced that they were getting engaged, they didn't seem to mind. Ed was reliable and independent and she could do a lot worse. They got married right after graduation, all the guests being on Fanny's side. Barton, his only friend, was his best man.

Fanny went to work at the general store in town and signed up for classes at the community college. It would take her a few years, but she would get her degree eventually if she plugged away at it. Ed got a job at the Granary Food Company in the stockroom. He didn't mind starting at the bottom because he was a hard worker and he knew something would happen sooner or later. Didn't do too badly, either. In three years he'd worked his way up to sales rep, which is funny when you come to think of it for a guy who didn't talk much, who didn't really like being around people. But sales was different. It wasn't personal, and he guessed all the stuff he'd learned being on his own made him bolder than he thought he'd be. Once a month he'd drive to Milwaukee, Madison, or Green Bay to talk to food wholesalers and retailers, trying to get them to increase their orders, talking up new products, arranging for distribution. He did his follow-up work by phone.

It was a relief to go home, even though Fanny was tired after work, particularly the nights she was at class. She didn't have the kind of energy she used to, but she still talked to him about her day. Sometimes he'd look over at her while she was standing at the stove, admiring the curve of her back and her strong calves, and he'd be surprised all over again that she was his wife. He whispered the word. "Wife."

He'd never had anyone before who seemed to care how he felt, who asked him how his day had gone. They still had fun together, going shopping, seeing a movie, getting together with her friends once in a while for dinner.

They'd been together three years when Keith was born, and Ed felt like a grownup for the first time. He wished his parents could see him now, a father, with a boy of his own, and a wife, a home, and a job. Even if the house was small and needed work, mortgage and all, it was still his. Ed set up a workshop in the basement, fixing things when he had the time, cleaning his guns, storing his knives and hunting gear. He bought a new recliner and found a magazine rack and a floor lamp at the Salvation Army. It was his own private space, something he'd never had before. When he got the money, he thought, he'd put in a wet bar down there.

Fanny's sewing room became the baby's. She took a leave from her job, which they promised she could have back when she was ready. She was the best worker they'd had, and they didn't want to lose her for good. She quit school, because there wasn't enough time now, and focused her energy on Keith.

She spent a lot of time in the house with him, more than Ed thought strictly necessary, especially once the baby had stopped nursing. She sang to him every night, old songs that she'd learned from her grandmother, who lived somewhere in the South. There was one song, her favorite, about a guy who abandoned his family and kids while he went off to do God's will, or what he thought was God's will. Then he died of the plague, leaving his children and everyone else mourning for him. He'd found it printed out once in an old shape-note hymn book Fanny had lying around. "The Lone Pilgrim," that was what it was called. He thought it was harsh and forlorn, hardly suitable for a child.

No, Fanny had said, it was a beautiful song, comforting. Her grandmother had sung it to her mother, her mother had sung it to her, and she was going to sing it to Keith.

Why, Ed insisted, couldn't she sing him normal lullabies?

That wasn't what she knew, she told him, and it wasn't any of his business anyways. If he had such a strong opinion about her choice, why didn't *he* sing the kid to sleep?

But he didn't let up. He gave her such a hard time every time he heard it that she eventually stopped singing altogether. But she still spent more time with the kid than she ever did with him. Late at night, she'd be sitting in the rocker reading while Keith slept, sometimes long after Ed had gone to bed.

When Ed got laid off, he wasn't all that surprised. He'd worked for the company for ten years. He didn't enjoy it, but he felt like he was holding his own, at least for a while. Then his regular customers started complaining that he wasn't paying attention to them, wasn't coming by often enough, was messing up the orders. He found himself gazing off into space while their voices became background noise, and then he'd have to ask them to repeat themselves. He didn't speak up much in meetings, just waited for someone else to make a suggestion, then nodded in agreement once he saw how the others were feeling about it. Small things started to annoy him, like when they were late bringing up the requisition slips from downstairs, or if someone didn't return his phone call right away. He didn't like the phone any more, always interrupting whatever he was doing. He wished there were a better way to do business. When the cutbacks came, he was the first to be let go.

For a while, when he was getting unemployment, it wasn't so bad. He could hunt as often as he wanted to, so long as he was home when Keith got back from school. He was seven, still too young to be left alone. Ed didn't mind, actually liked it. He would make Keith a peanut butter and jelly sandwich, sit with him while he did his homework. Sometimes Keith would ask Ed to read to him, but Ed told him he was too old for that kind of thing.

Fanny was getting edgy, though. She was always after him, asking him had he read the want ads, had he called any of the people whose names she'd suggested, friends of her father's, who might have ideas about work? What exactly was he doing with his day, she wanted to know. At least if he made dinner it would take a little of the load off her, she suggested, but he never learned how to cook, and as she pointed out all the time, it didn't look like he was about to start.

It was almost a year before he started working again, this time on the assembly line at the plant in Sauk City, making gear boxes for their fork lifts. He was fast, always had been good with his hands. He didn't have to talk to anyone, and he got a steady check, even if it was a whole lot less than he'd gotten at GFC. In the lunchroom, whenever one of the boys acted friendly, Ed would scowl, make it clear that he wasn't the social type. He'd rather be left alone.

Ed didn't mind when he came home to an empty house. A lot of the time Keith was playing at a friend's after school, and sometimes he stayed overnight. Fanny worked late a lot, too. She was managing the store now, and after it closed for the day she did inventory and billing and other stuff that she said she didn't have time for otherwise. She'd leave him a TV dinner, sometimes a leftover piece of meatloaf and some potatoes that he could heat up. He'd take his food and a beer downstairs to the recliner, put his feet up, and read. He had a stack of magazines, *Field and Stream, Midwest Outdoors, Shotgun News, Trapper*, and *Predator Caller*, some books on turkey and deer hunting that he'd sent away for.

The quiet didn't bother him—in fact, he preferred it. It was better for his blood pressure anyhow. He was taking his medicine, but he was sure that he'd feel better if he could spend more time alone, not talking, not having to be around other people. They were always interrupting him. How was he supposed to get anything done? On the assembly line, a friendly comment could cause him to lose his pace, mess up his rhythm. Off the line, he didn't want anyone interfering with his breaks. He just wanted to be still for a minute, drink his coffee, get on with it.

At home it was the same thing. Whenever he got comfortable, Fanny was sure to ask him a question. He'd be peacefully cleaning his guns, and she'd want to know if he'd remembered to take the garbage out. If he was downstairs practicing his calls, she'd open the basement door and yell down wanting to know had he fixed the rain gutter on the side of the house, did he bring in the firewood, had he taken the meat out of the freezer. If he sat down at the kitchen table for a minute to drink a beer, Keith would wander in, asking him for money, griping that here was nothing to do in Leland and wanting to know if he'd drive him to town, a half hour away. Sometimes he'd ignore them, hoping they'd go away. Sometimes he'd mutter, "Can't you see I'm busy? Ask me later, for Chrissake." In his head, though, he was yelling, "Leave me the fuck alone, why can't you?"

It seemed like Fanny was bitching at him all the time. "That television is so damned loud I can't hear myself think," she'd yell from the kitchen.

"Why is it always me who has to get up in the middle of the night when Keith has one of his nightmares?" she'd complain. "I work too, you know. I need my sleep just as bad as you do."

Sometimes he'd turn to find her staring at him, an exasperated look on her face. "Why are you ignoring me?" she'd ask. "Whenever it's something you don't want to do, you just pretend I don't exist. I'm sick and tired of how you only pay attention when it suits you."

Fanny had been harping about his hearing, insisting that he should see a specialist. "You don't hear the dog barking to be let out," she said. "I come home and find a pile of shit by the door. Half the time you can't even hear the phone ringing." Her voice softened. "Ed, please, go get it checked out. What harm would it do?"

"There's nothing wrong with me that a little peace and quiet won't fix," he insisted. "Just leave me alone, why don't you?"

She just wouldn't let go. "It's for your own good," she insisted. "Don't you want to know what's going on around you?"

"I'll tell you what the fuck is wrong," he finally said, jaw clenched. "The reception on the fucking TV is bad, always has been. You're the one who doesn't want to spend the money on a satellite dish, not me." He paused to take a breath. "And what the hell is Keith having nightmares for, at his age? He'd get over them soon enough if you didn't go running to him every time he got scared."

Once in a while, after Sunday dinner, his stomach full of roast chicken and gravy, he'd look over at Fanny, wondering what had happened to that bubbly laugh, to all those friends, all her projects. She'd put on some weight, and she never wore lipstick any more. Cut off her hair, too. She said it was too much trouble to keep it long.

A couple of times he suggested going to a movie at the mall.

"I'm too tired to think," she told him, "much less go out."

He tried asking again on the weekend. "That's when I have to do the shopping and cleaning, and it isn't as though you're any help in that department either," she said. All she seemed to want to do was read, or once in a while play Scrabble with Keith. Sometimes he'd find the two of them curled up on the couch with their books, a bowl of chips between them.

She'd stopped asking him when he was going to see a doctor about his hearing. When he told her that someone at the lunch counter started cursing him out because he didn't know the guy was asking him to pass the ketchup, she just shrugged.

On the evening of their thirteenth wedding anniversary, she told him she was leaving. She was standing in the living room, a cup of coffee in her hand, looking out at the dark. He looked up from his magazine, confused.

"What did you say?" he asked, annoyed. He could hear a faint drone, maybe cicadas, but it sounded as though it were coming from inside his head instead of out there in the yard.

"I'm leaving," she repeated, louder. "It's not that you forgot our anniversary, because you always forget it, nothing new there."

He jumped. Shit, he thought, I did it again. How the hell am I supposed to remember every little thing? "So what, then?" he asked. "It's not as though I don't do my share, pay most of the bills, fix things around here. I'm not some fucking drunk, or gambler. So what is it? You want Prince Charming?"

"I can't stand feeling like a stranger in my own house, like I'm an intruder," she said, not turning around. Her fingers fumbled with the scallop on the curtain's edge. "Every time you see me, you look annoyed. You never talk to me any more, we never do anything together. When's the last time we had sex?"

"Well, whose fault is that?" Ed retorted. "I ask you to go to the movies and you're too goddamn tired. You're too tired to even cook a meal, except for Sunday. I'm eating out of the fucking freezer, is what's happening. And if I ever even touch you, you turn your back on me. Whose fault is that?"

She sighed. "Keith is the only thing we have in common," she said, her eyes reddening, "and all we do is fight about how to raise him. I'm sorry," she said, "I just can't do this any more."

"Ok, if it's so important to you, I'll call the doctor," he said. "I'll get the name of the hearing guy."

"It's too late," she said, turning away in the gloom. "I've made up my mind."

He didn't do anything about his hearing, not right away. Fanny was leaving anyway, so what difference did it make? He was out hunting with Barton early one morning when he realized that he couldn't track the birds any more. His calls were as good as ever, but he caught Barton looking at him funny when he wondered out loud why they didn't respond.

When he got home, he went to his desk and rifled through the papers, trying to find the name of the doctor. It turned up on the back of an old bill.

The good news, they said, was that they could do something about it. The bad news, at least according to Ed, was that he'd have to wear a hearing aid. Now everyone would know that he was deaf. On the other hand, hearing aids had changed, they were so small now you could barely see them, and maybe no one would notice. They worked, too. You could adjust the sound for one-on-one conversation, for a noisy restaurant, for the movies, and it would switch frequencies automatically when you were talking on the phone.

When he came back from the dealer's, he had the volume control in his shirt pocket and the earpieces snugly in each ear. They didn't show, really, and he could always grow his hair longer if he felt self-conscious about them. He needed to play around with the thing, they said, till he figured out how to use all its features. It couldn't be any more complicated than programming the VCR. He'd figure it out in his own good time. The first thing he wanted to do was get out in the woods and see how it worked for hunting.

Too bad about Keith. He would have liked to have him along. But the crybaby obviously had better things to do. The thought came and left.

There was a faint crackle, like static. He turned the buttons slowly. He could hear the wind in the trees for the first time in years. It was familiar but eerie, too. He was hiking a logging road deep into the woods, the pines towering overhead, the air crisp. It was going to be a good day, he could feel it. He stepped off the path, then followed a rise to where he had a 180 degree view of the landscape. He turned his attention to the hills in front of him, and began to call the hens softly. He thought he could hear a response from the right, and turned slowly to see what was doing. A couple of hens crossed the crest of the hill, moving fast, but he couldn't see anything else. Then he heard another sound, a kind of low hum, that seemed to be coming from the hearing aid. He shook his head sharply, and the noise stopped.

In the distance, very faintly, he could hear a melody, snatches of a song that he thought he knew. A woman's voice was singing slowly, high and thin. "*I came to the place where the lone pilgrim lay . . .*" A sad song. It sounded like Fanny's voice, but he couldn't be sure. Yes, it was. It was the song she used to sing to Keith when he was little.

He listened again. It was so faint he could barely hear it, but it was there. The notes flew up and down, moved around like wind whistling through the trees. It was a lonesome sound, all right.

"*When in a lone whisper I heard something say, 'how sweetly I sleep here alone',*" the voice sang.

He drew his lips together, pressed them down hard. When you were dead maybe sleep would be sweet, but you wouldn't know it because you'd be dead. He had been sleeping alone for two years now, and he wouldn't exactly call it sweet, either. Wouldn't even call it sleep. He was up and down all night, needing to take a leak, trying to get comfortable, tossing from side to side, having bad dreams. He'd dream that Fanny was back, her soft breath on his chest, and he'd feel peaceful, lying there, glad that she'd come to her senses after all. Then something would happen and he'd wake up in his dream and she'd be gone. As soon as he felt that sick lurch, knowing she'd left, he'd wake up for real and know that she was gone all over again. He wanted her to get out of his head, to leave his fucking dreams alone. He wished there was a shut-off valve for dreams, a switch next to the on/off button on his hearing aid that he could push when he was about to go to bed. A dreamless sleep. He wanted to turn his mind off altogether.

The song had stopped, or he couldn't hear it any more. He turned his attention back to the birds, starting his calls again. The hearing aid worked okay, because he could hear a gobbler yelp way off to the right, next to a stand of trees. He sat down on his vest pad, his back against a large tree, and loaded his gun, thinking about its heft and balance. He'd tried to convince Barton that the .12-gauge with a super-full choke and a good load could do everything a .10 could, with less weight and recoil to boot. Barton just shook his head, said he wasn't about to wear a sissy-pad to keep his shoulder from turning into mush, and he preferred to use a .20-gauge, which Ed thought of as a beginner gun. Ed's own shoulder was just fine, he thought with satisfaction, and the more you use a big load, the tougher your shoulder gets.

He pulled his shotgun up and took aim. As he breathed out, he pressed the trigger, and the bird went down. "All right!" he yelled, feeling the surge of triumph he always felt when he bagged one. His shout echoed in the woods. Then, just behind him, he heard Keith.

"Dad, listen," Keith said. Or did he? Ed swiveled. No one there. He reached into his hunting vest and made another adjustment to the box. His son's voice was urgent and plaintive, but the words were hard to make out. He thought he heard him say "I'm scared," but he couldn't be sure.

Ed felt the hairs on the back of his neck go up. Had Keith changed his mind and decided to come at the last minute? But Ed was alone, there was no one else around.

He started to panic and fumbled for the off switch on the box. What had he heard? Was it some kind of weird radio frequency? Was it like a cell phone or something? Or was it his imagination? It was Keith all right, but where was he, and why was he talking like that? He sounded tentative and sad, not sullen like he usually did.

Ed turned the hearing aid on again, and tried to listen over his rapid breathing, but there was nothing. My imagination, he thought, just my imagination. He started up the hill to pick up his kill.

It was late morning, and the sun was slanting high up through the trees. The air was cool, and he could hear the birds and small animals and crickets. It was odd, he realized, because for years now he'd been enjoying the silence of the woods, and all of a sudden now they were noisy. Birds made a real racket. His footsteps crunched loudly underneath him. He decided to turn the hearing aid off for a while, at least till after he'd had his lunch.

The bird was big, a twenty-pounder at least. He cut the beard off, used his pruning shears to clip the legs and spurs, then field-dressed it, discarding the innards and rinsing the cavity with water from a nearby stream. Then he packed it away in the pouch he carried at the back of his camo vest.

He found a shady spot and sat down on the grass, pulling a cheese sandwich and a thermos of coffee from his backpack. He had a candy bar and a small flask in there too, for later. He peeled the waxed paper off and took a bite. The mustard was sharp on his tongue, and the bread was a little stale. What the hell, he thought, it doesn't make any difference, it tastes fine. He hadn't been in the mood to go into the store, risk running into Fanny. He didn't want to see her any more than he had to. Keith either.

He lay down on his back in the grass, shutting his eyes. He was tired, he realized, hadn't slept well again. He yawned and let himself doze off.

Fanny's voice was whispering faintly in his ear. "Eddie, Eddie," she was saying, "Come home."

He sat bolt upright, trying to focus. It sounded like Fanny, but she definitely wasn't out here in the woods. She never went out with him, swore she never would. Now he was really spooked. He took out the volume control and checked, but it was still off. He tested the switch, on, off, on, off, then jiggled the knob. If he was imagining things, he was in trouble. He'd never heard voices before, never had any reason to doubt his own sanity. He was a little deaf, sure, but that didn't make him nuts. He coughed, loudly, then tentatively made a call, a little purr-purr, like he did to rouse the hens.

There it was again, the singing, faint but definitely there. It seemed to be coming from someplace closer in. He shivered. Shit, he told himself, he wasn't going to let it get to him. He realized with a start that he was afraid. The music was bad enough, but the words to the damned song were really creepy. Here's this guy who died of the fucking plague, all alone on the road somewhere. He could hear Fanny more clearly now. "*He wandered an exile and stranger from home,*" she sang, "*no kindred or relative nigh . . .*"

That was him, all right. He didn't belong anywhere, no family, didn't have a home anymore either. Closest thing to it was out here in the woods, alone, just him and the birds. He knew the birds as well as he knew himself, but they weren't exactly his friends. He was out there to kill them, no matter how seductive his mating calls, how sociable the clucks and yelps that would gather the toms together in a fit of male bonding.

Up ahead he thought he saw something move. Not a turkey, though. Maybe another hunter. Keith? He whistled, then said out loud, "Anyone there?"

He heard Keith's voice again. "You didn't want to talk to me."

"That's not true," Ed shot back without thinking. "I tried, but you never had any time, never wanted to work on models or learn about guns or try out my calling reeds. I couldn't even get you to sit down and watch a little TV with me, for Chrissake." He looked around him, startled. Fuck, here he was, talking to the trees. What the hell was the matter with him?

"Too late, Dad," Keith said.

Ed could feel a strange sensation deep in his gut, like sandpaper rubbing the inside of his stomach. He felt like choking the kid. "Oh yeah?" he yelled, suddenly angry, "is that what you think, you little wimp? You never had any balls, you piece of shit. You're a mama's boy, always were."

He thought he heard Fanny again, admonishing him.

He turned on his heel, glaring at the trees behind him. "You too, you fat cow," he yelled. "All you ever cared about was him. You never even gave me the time of day once he came along. Too tired, my ass. Get away from me, both of you."

He turned and gathered up his gear, putting the remains of his lunch away, emptying the dregs of the coffee onto the ground. Before he closed his pack, he unscrewed the flask and took a deep swallow. The whiskey burned. He took one more, just to be sure, and put it away. It was getting cold out anyhow, and it would warm him up. It was quiet, now, and the light was just starting to fade. He thought he'd better be getting back.

As Ed walked rapidly back toward the trail, he felt a little calmer. The woods were so peaceful at dusk, the deep blue shadows taking on more substance than the foliage. Tall branches swayed in the wind, making shifting patterns of light on the forest floor. The ground was covered with leaves that shivered like pale feathers on either side of the path. He thought maybe he'd cook the turkey up, make a stew this time instead of throwing the bird into the big freezer in the basement. He wasn't going to be able to fit that much more in there anyhow. He should give some of it to the ladies over at the Church. They could use it for the next Church supper, or make sausage for one of their pancake breakfasts.

Ed steadied himself. He had no idea what had happened back there, but he wasn't nuts. He'd always had a pretty solid grip on things. He'd read an article in the paper a while back, about stress. They said that it could make some strange stuff happen. Stress could affect your blood pressure, which was a problem with him. Come to think of it, it might even be the medication he was taking to keep it under control. Maybe it could make you hear things that weren't there. He would call the doctor, make sure he wasn't taking too much of it. He picked up speed, suddenly wanting to get home. Maybe he'd give Barton a ring, see what he was up to.

It was getting darker, and when he looked up he could see the stars. The tops of the trees were silhouetted against the sky. They looked like they were waving to him.

He'd slowed down, trying to catch his breath, when the notes rang out again, directly in front of him. He wasn't going to stop to listen, no way. He pushed ahead, his body leaning into the current of sound. "*The tempest may howl, and the loud thunder roar . . .*" Fanny sang, her voice clean and certain, pushing at him, meeting him headlong. "*And gathering storms may arise . . .*" He tried to walk faster, but he couldn't avoid it, the sound curling around his head and shoulders, wrapping him in its net.

He stopped, terrified, and peered anxiously into the woods. In the gloom, he made out a tree stump, and moving jerkily toward it, threw his pack down and pulled it open, frantically searching for the flask. As his fingers closed around the cool metal, he told himself that it was nothing, just a bad memory, that's all, he'd be home soon and pull himself together, call Barton to come over early. Taking a deep breath, Ed tilted his head back and let the liquor burn its way down his throat. This shit had to stop. He'd make it stop. But something dark was building deep in his chest.

He reached into his vest and yanked the little box out of the pocket where he'd put it, hurling it in one clean, furious arc against the nearest tree, where it bounced off the bark with a ping and landed on the grass. Frantic now, Ed grabbed his shotgun, lifted it to his shoulder and aimed. The box shattered, shards flying. He walked over to the place where it had fallen, looked down at the small tangle of wires, then took his shotgun butt and bashed in what remained of it. Then he remembered, and yanked the earpieces out. He threw them down and smashed them, too.

"Don't fuck with me, don't ever fuck with me again if you know what's good for you," he screamed, enraged. His heart was pounding, hurting his ribs.

"*Yet calm are his feelings, at rest is his soul, the tears are all wiped from his eyes . . .*" The voice shimmered, fell away, then delicately swooped up again, the words round and smooth as pearls. One after the other they fell into place, as if they were strung on a silver thread. Suddenly it was silent again. The wind had died down, and there was a faint ringing in his ears.

He sat down on the stump, putting his gun down carefully beside him. He could feel something moving up from his chest to his throat, a gelatinous, egg-shaped mass, cold and nauseating. It lodged there, taking the wind out of him. He choked, coughing, as the lump exploded from his throat in one tremendous sob that tore at his chest and stomach, contracted his lungs, catapulted his heart back against his ribs. The sob ended in a high, thin sound, the kind an animal makes when a trap snaps shut on its body, clamping through bone and sinew.

Nailed

I always wanted to be an artist, a desire my Polish Catholic family considered only slightly less tragic than the Warsaw Uprising. They'd left Wadowice for America just in time.

"*Sztuka*! Art! What good is that?" my mother was constantly asking. "Is foolish, no use for anything." She would sigh as if her heart was going to heave up out of her chest. "I don't know what to do with you, Krystyna, so stubborn." She was right. But art was the one thing I truly cared about. Well, that and Jimmy. He was tall and wiry, with a shock of long brown hair and a grin that showed off the gap in his front teeth as though it were a prize. Unlike the other boys, he always looked me straight in the eye. That look said I was the only thing he ever wanted to look at again. We met sitting next to each other the first day of eighth grade at Saint Stanislaus Kostka in Brooklyn, and from then on we were inseparable. Art was the only rival Jimmy ever had, and he was the only person in my life who never seemed to mind my obsession.

From the time I was little, I drew on any surface that was handy. My mother was always yelling at me when she found doodles on the kitchen table, or later on when I made tiny, detailed pencil drawings on the wall next to my bed. Then one day in April, our seventh grade class went on a trip to the city, to the Metropolitan Museum. I remember those enormous steps, and the feeling at the top like we were going into a church. It was so huge I worried that I'd get separated from the others and miss the bus home. It nearly happened, too, because I stopped to stare at a big painting in a gold frame—"Annunciation," the label said—with an angel and rays of light and people in long robes holding books. When I looked up the others were gone. But I caught up with them two galleries ahead. There were so many kids that nobody had even noticed I'd been missing.

I swore I'd go back to that museum on my own because I had to look at those angel wings again—red and gold and blue and green and colors that I didn't even have names for. And the backgrounds! I wanted to fall into the paintings in that room, explore the hills and little houses, ride the tiny hay cart behind a straining donkey, climb to the top of a tall, thin tower and peer through its battlements at the turquoise sky.

I began filling my school notebooks and pieces of scrap paper with careful drawings, trying to capture the sheen of an eye or the playfulness of one of the little dogs that followed the donkey cart. I discovered that if I made my images small, really small, my imagination could slide into them more easily, and they looked better on the page too, because you couldn't see the mistakes as well.

I begged my mother to take me back to the museum, but she gave me one of her looks. "What for you wanna go to a museum?" she said. "Plenty to do here, plenty to see. You waste your time, always drawing, drawing."

"It's not wasting time, Mama," I insisted. "It's what I'm good at."

"Is gonna make you a living? Get you a husband?" My mother's comments were as unvarying as her Thursday night kielbasa. So were my responses. I was only twelve, and thinking about getting married was on the same plane as becoming an astronaut. As for a job, I already had one. I baby-sat every Friday and Saturday night for Mrs. Nowak, so she and her husband could go to the dances in the basement of our church.

It didn't take long for me to be able to get to the museum on my own. It wasn't that complicated a subway ride from Greenpoint. I went on Sunday afternoons, when my mother thought I was at the library studying. I mostly hung out in the early Flemish galleries, sitting on the floor with my sketchpads and pencils as I struggled to reproduce the intricate patterning of a gown or a tiled floor in one of those amazing altarpieces. By the time I was in high school, I had been there longer than most of the guards.

One of my favorite paintings was a portrait of a young man in black, with a sparse, wiry little beard, a painting that I felt like eating, that was how much I wanted it to be part of me. The man's face was lively and smart, and he looked a lot like Jimmy, if you took off the beard and the funny flat hat and lace collar, and put a motorcycle helmet and leather jacket on him.

My parents complained about how much time I spent on my "hobby," as they called it. They shouldn't have been surprised—it was probably genetic. My dad was particularly good at *wycinanki*, the traditional craft of paper cutting, and he prided himself on his skill with the sheep shears, which were always used for that particular art form. He was also great at *pisanki*, painting eggs in bright colors and intricate designs for Easter. He was a supervisor at the Post Office, a big step up from working at the family grocery store in the old country, but he always found time for his hobby. So why did they give me such a hard time? Probably because they couldn't see how I could make a living out of it.

All through high school, in addition to baby-sitting, I worked at the Pink

Palace Beauty Salon on Driggs Avenue, about a ten minute walk from our house. Rose Woźniak, the owner, was easy-going and generous, and she liked me, so every afternoon—from 3:30 to 6:30, except Sunday when the store was closed, and Saturday when I was there all day—I washed hair, swept up, answered the phone, got the ladies their coffee, whatever needed doing. Even though my mother couldn't argue with the money I was making, she complained that I'd never meet a man working in a beauty parlor. I ignored her, because I couldn't imagine being with anyone but Jimmy.

He told me all the time that I was a great artist, that there was no present in the world he'd rather have than one of my drawings. There was nothing he wouldn't do for me, even saving up to buy me expensive brushes and watercolors. But my parents made it clear from the start that he was not a suitable match. Maybe they felt superior because Jimmy's dad was a janitor and his mom took in laundry and sewing. And they had five kids, while I was an only child.

They hated his long hair, his leather jacket, his shyness. Or maybe it was just that they didn't like the thought of what we might be doing together. They didn't know that we had agreed to wait until we got married, after graduation, to go all the way. That's how much we loved each other.

They also didn't like the fact that Jimmy wanted to be a musician and spent most of his free time practicing guitar and playing in the band that he and his friends had started. I loved to watch his beautiful long fingers when he played. It was as if they had a life of their own, completely unrelated to the person they belonged to. Jimmy promised that when they cut their first album, I'd be the one to do the cover. Their music was different, a radical new sound with roots in hip-hop, heavy metal, and reggae, and gorgeous lyrics about what the world could become if people cared enough to change it. Without ever actually hearing his music, my parents called it "noise." I called it art.

When you're happy, you think it will last forever. It was a beautiful Saturday afternoon in October, our last year of school, and I had just turned seventeen. I'd been waiting for Jimmy on the corner after work. He was picking me up to take me to dinner and a movie. I saw him coming down the street on his BSA, and when he spotted me he smiled and waved, turning the bike toward the curb where I was standing. Only thing was, he turned right in the path of a Lincoln town car that was speeding to the airport. I heard the squeal of brakes, and then I saw Jimmy's body fly up into the air like a javelin, turning to land head first with a little bounce, flattening and settling into the asphalt in slow motion. I knew before I got there that he was gone.

My parents went with me to the funeral and made all the right noises, but I knew that deep down they were relieved that he was out of the way.

The grief I felt kept me jackknifed in bed, sobbing, asking God why he had taken Jimmy away. What had I done to be punished like that? Maybe if I had waited in front of the shop instead of at the corner, the accident wouldn't have happened. I wanted out of the world, away from my family's constantly telling me I'd get over it, that I was only a teenager and I just needed to let some time pass. If I couldn't be with Jimmy, there wasn't any reason to be there at all. But as much as I wanted to die, I didn't have the nerve to do that to my family. I kept picturing their faces when they learned that I'd jumped in front of a train or thrown myself off the roof of our building. I only stopped thinking about dying when I discovered the Persian miniatures at the museum. I started going there all the time, and that's what saved me.

When I graduated from high school in June, my mother really started harping on me. "How you gonna find somebody if you spend all your time hiding in that museum?" It was her theme song, morning and night, whenever she had me within earshot. But I was out of the house during the day now, working full time at the salon. My father, annoyed at her endless whining, joined her mission, thinking it might speed things up, convince me sooner. He wanted to know why I didn't go to beauty school or secretarial school or learn dressmaking and get a decent job, especially if I wasn't even going to make the effort to look for a new guy.

"*Tata*," I told him, "I am not going to run the risk of losing someone I love ever again."

"You gotta get over him," my father insisted. "Is not good for you to be sad like this."

Sad? If that's what they wanted to call it, fine. My heart was shattered and it wasn't going to be glued back together no matter how much they insisted. But they kept telling me that I needed to get out more, change my attitude, see things differently.

So I did. I bought a 1993 Kawasaki Vulcan, six-speed transmission, bright red, in great condition. When I rode it, I felt as though the world dropped away, and my worries with it. And I felt connected to Jimmy.

When I told them about the motorcycle, my family acted like hell had opened up under them. My mother wept and my father paced. My aunts and uncles pleaded with me.

"You know what happened to Jimmy," they said. "You wanna send your parents to an early grave?"

"*Chciałabym umrzeć.* I wish I was dead," my mother moaned.

"Why do you have to do this?" they kept asking. Even my cousin Zuza, a freshman at Brooklyn College and usually my loyal ally, didn't understand. She pulled me into a corner one night during a surface-to-surface missile attack disguised as a family dinner. "What's the matter with a car, for God's sake?" she asked.

"Parking," I said.

"No, this is about Jimmy," she insisted. "It's your way of keeping him alive."

"What's so terrible about that?" I asked.

"You'll never look at anybody else, is what." Zuza shook her head, her lips making a sad, thin line across her face. I gave her a conciliatory hug, and looked around for an escape route, but I was trapped at the long dinner table between her and my aunt Lydia.

The more they badgered me, the more desperate I was to get away, and I decided that art school was the answer. I read all the catalogs I could find, figured out which courses I wanted to take, even filled out applications to Parsons, Pratt, and the School of Visual Arts. But I never sent them in, because I knew that I was only dreaming. There was no way I could get that amount of money together, and a scholarship was out of the question. I'd been a mediocre student because my school life was Jimmy and nothing but Jimmy, and I hadn't even bothered to take the SATs.

My mother kept harping on me, wanting to know what was wrong. Finally, I told her. "I want to go to art school," I said, "but I can't afford it."

"What for?" she asked, astonished. She threw her hands up, and turned back to the sink. When it came to art, my mother had only one response.

I gave up. They were right, all those dreams were just so much hot air. Time to get real. I signed up at The Brooklyn Institute of Beauty Sciences for a manicure course, because it was something I thought I could make a living at. It wasn't all that hard, but there was a lot to learn. I did paraffin wax treatments, silk wraps, overlays, and tip application, taking time out to cry in the bathroom. I learned transfers, stencils, dust and striping techniques, and I slept twelve hours a night, I was so depressed. I took an airbrushing course that taught me to blend color, use acrylic paints instead of nail varnish, even produce my own designs, which for me was like selling hot dogs on the street instead of a being a chef at a good restaurant.

It took me over seven months and about three grand, but I passed the State Board exams and they signed me up at the Pink Palace. I had given up my visits to the Museum, because I was too busy. Maybe my mother was right. What was the use of doing something so impractical? It wasn't going to get me anywhere except more depressed.

I was still living at home, because I had to pay off my tuition loan. My parents had settled down, to the extent that my mother no longer burst into tears whenever she saw me, and my father actually talked to me about something besides my mother's complaints. I was just starting to accept that this was what my life was going to be, and I even began to enjoy the routine, as long as they left me alone.

Then one day after work I came in and found my mother in the living room with a short skinny guy who looked like Tony Bennett, only with a lot less hair. And my mother was smiling, which was the tip-off. She had gotten it in her head to arrange a marriage for me. Not that she was going to tell me about anything so old-world—she was just going to find someone, talk to the boy's parents, set it all up, and then get us together.

"*Kochanie*, darling," she said, "I want you to meet Piotr. I mean, Peter. He's here from Pennsylvania, where he goes to school." She turned to peer at him coyly. "Accounting, right?" He sprang to his feet and shook my hand as though it had a jump rope instead of my arm attached to it.

I couldn't help glaring at him, but my mother had me pinned like an insect smack in the middle of her only frame of reference.

"Sit down, *Krysia*," my mother said. "Have a glass of tea. You and Peter should get to know each other. His parents are from Kraków, too."

What she meant was, "Either sit down, or call the ambulance to take me to the hospital." So I sat down. Actually, he wasn't all that bad. He had a nice laugh, and he'd actually set foot inside a museum once—the Museum of Natural History. But after fifteen minutes of small talk, it was all I could do to keep myself from jumping out of the window. I finally looked up at my mother and said, "I'm sorry, *Mamo*, I have to go. I'm supposed to baby sit tonight, and I'm late already." It was a lie, but I was desperate. My mother looked as though I'd slapped her.

I felt bad, so I gave in a little. "Peter," I said, "why don't you walk me out?" I grabbed my leather jacket and helmet off the coat stand, gave my mother a warning look and fled, Peter racing down the stairs behind me. Once safely outside, I unlocked the Kawasaki and turned to him.

"You're a nice person, and I don't want to disappoint you—or her," I said. "But my fiancé was killed in an accident a year and a half ago, and I'm just not ready for another relationship. I don't think I will be, either, for a very long time."

He gave me a dejected look and shook my hand again, a little less enthusiastically than before. "Well," he said, "if you change your mind . . ."

I nodded, leapt on the bike, and roared off without offering him a ride.

The following day, my father sat me down. "*Krysiu*," he said, "you're killing your mother. She can't sleep. She got pains in her chest worrying about you. She don't understand, you're nineteen already, before you know, you're gonna be too old. You don't wanna spend your life in the beauty parlor. Why don't you at least let your mother try? There's lotsa nice young fellas in the neighborhood."

"I'm not interested in meeting any men," I said. "If I have any free time at all, I'd rather spend it drawing. But I don't."

He sighed, sounding exactly like my mother, and went back to reading his *Gazeta Wyborcza*.

At work, at least, things were going well. Manicures themselves were boring, but I started enjoying decorating the nails once they were done. Once I was confident of my technical skills, I decided to branch out.

My first guinea pig was Mrs. Nemojewski, who came in every Saturday at ten with Aza, her Pekingese lap dog, to have her hair and nails done and her upper lip waxed. Her wrinkled hands had big joints and brown freckles all over the backs of them, but she was fanatical about her nails, long silk-wrapped talons that curved over the ends of her fingers. Once I'd convinced her to take the first baby step away from solid red polish to an airbrushed design on her ring finger, she was hooked.

"I have a great idea," I whispered conspiratorially one Saturday. "If you don't like it, you don't have to pay me." That cinched the deal. I made her promise not to look while I was doing it, which was no problem because as always, she was busy gabbing with her friends in the other chairs. When I was done and I finally let her see it, her jaw dropped. She had an exquisite miniature Aza on the thumbnail of her right hand. She stared at her nail, then at me, then at Aza, then back at her nail. She paid me twenty dollars with an extra five thrown in for a tip, and went over to share her marvel with her pals.

Overnight, I had more appointments than I could handle, for painted miniatures of the ladies' pets, then their grandchildren. I was moving up in the nail world. The better I got at my work, the more adventurous my ladies became, too. One of them asked me to paint a picture of her new sofa. Another wanted her window box, full of colorful flowers and trailing vines. One of my aunts arrived with a package, unwrapping a prized china cup and saucer that she wanted me to reproduce. Even Zuza came by, asking me if I could give her the New York skyline at night. Before long, we had to start booking customers weeks in advance.

My mother still complained, but once she saw my work on her friends, her curiosity got the better of her and she came by the shop to see me in action. Before I knew it, she was there almost every day, setting out my tools, cleaning them, helping to book my appointments.

Then the *Daily News* showed up at the Pink Palace, wanting to do a story. Rose was thrilled, because it was good for business, but that was just the beginning. *Cosmo* ran a feature on my work, with a picture of me with my head bent over old Mrs. Dudek's left hand, busy with a family portrait commission—her mother and her grandmother, on the fore- and ring fingers. Two portraits take a long time, just over three hours, so my ladies have to make sure to go to the bathroom ahead of time, and be able to hold it until the nails are really dry.

I'm not at the Palace any more. An electronic music diva named Sue Cee saw my stuff in *New York* magazine and called me. She loved looking at art as much as I did, and wanted to see if I could do something from one of Goya's black paintings for her. Depressing, but why not? Might as well push the envelope. I chose the one of Saturn and his son, with his eyes all popping out, about to chomp on the bloody, decapitated figure of his own kid. It was a detail, just the giant's bearded head and shoulders and part of the body he was eating, and it came out really well. That was during Sue's own black period, which lasted about a year. Now I'm doing early Flemish scenes for her, and we're both happy.

For a couple of years, now I've had my own business doing custom work—

house calls only, for which my clients pay me a lot. Enough to have bought my folks a bigger house in the old neighborhood, and pay off the rest of Rose's mortgage on her shop—and to get myself a small loft in downtown Manhattan. The person who does my books is Peter Dubrow, the entertainment industry's new hotshot accountant—the guy my mother once tried to fix me up with. Most of my clientele is in the music world, rock 'n' roll divas, even an opera star or two. I also have a few clients in the movie biz, and recently I've added a couple of heavy-duty socialites. Because so many of my regulars are always on the road, I get to fly out to L.A. or sometimes even to Europe. I stay at nice places, eat in good restaurants, drive around in the limos they send for me. My father says I always had a good business head. He brags that my artistic talents obviously come from his side of the family, and pulls out his own work to prove it.

My mother is working full time at the front desk at Rose's now, in addition to doing all of my bookings. She likes the money I make, but it doesn't stop her from complaining. Recently, I overheard her telling my Aunt Lydia that that if I'd gone to art school, I surely would have met somebody and been married by now. I had to laugh.

"She is not a young chicken any more," my mother continued. "Work keeps her so busy she don't have time for anything else."

My mother sighed like she was exhaling for the last time. "She will find a husband when she's ready," she said with finality, as though the statement itself guaranteed results.

That's what *she* thinks, but I'm not at all convinced she's right.

On the other hand, I'm not so sure she's wrong, either.

BETWEEN US

The sheet has slipped down and twisted around my legs, where it's got a death grip on my ankle. I open my eyes and look over at the window. The glass is a dull gray. Hard to tell what time it is, exactly, but I know it's early. Too early. The mail isn't going to arrive at 6:00 a.m. Or seven, or even eight. In Manhattan, it sometimes doesn't show up till three in the afternoon.

I turn over, trying to push the offending sheet off with my free foot. I bump Amy with my hip, kind of by accident, but she doesn't move. She always sleeps that way, not a sound, not a twitch, not a sign that she's even alive—that is, until she finally wakes up, all systems go, leaping out of bed with whistles and bells and sirens blaring. Watching her always makes me feel like going back to bed.

I yawn, start to stretch. The pain stops me before I get too far. It's been almost six months, but it still pinches where the stitches were, even when I'm not moving. I have to be careful not to pull or put too much pressure on the scars. Every once in a while I forget, and wham, it's like the skin is tearing from the inside. If I look down—and mostly, I try not to—I see a network of ridges and canals, back roads and railroad tracks. My chest looks like a Civil War battle map, showing the deployment of troops, the fields where skirmishes took place, territory was lost, borders redrawn, soldiers died.

I've been waiting for the package forever. They said it would take a while, four to six weeks, maybe even longer, because it was made to order. I've been on the web site so many times I can navigate it by heart, and I also know that there's no rushing it. It's going to arrive in its own good time. I want it to be today.

I ease myself out of bed and shuffle into the bathroom to pee. I hate to pee because I have to sit down to do it, but there it is. There's that paper cone they make that directs the stream from the wide part out the narrow end, so that women can do it standing. But I'm not interested.

I don't like looking in the mirror, either. I have short, thick hair, cut blunt, with a cowlick that I smooth down every morning with water, even though I know it's going to pop up again in five minutes. If it really annoys me, I'll dab on some Brylcreem and rake a comb through it. My jaw is too small. So are my ears. They're the kind that women long for but that I hate, they're so round, so perfect, like a doll's. I have narrow hips and a flat belly, which is good, but I tend to slump. When I was twelve, I got into the habit of crossing my arms over my chest, trying to hide what was there. I'm almost forty, but I still stand that way.

I shower at night so I can get up and out early in the morning. I can't stand being late, so I make sure it doesn't happen. I can get dressed in seven minutes flat, including brushing my teeth. First the straps, then my cotton underpants, grey trousers, grey shirt and matching black-and-grey tie. I shove my feet into my oxfords and move to the kitchen. Amy doesn't hear the drawers opening and closing, doesn't hear me grunt when I bend down to tie my shoes.

I pour water into the coffee pot and measure out the dark roast we keep in the freezer, then plug it in. The pot gurgles twice and settles down to business. I'm looking up at the clock, but there's plenty of time, no problem. I grab a handful of breakfast cereal from the box and cram it into my mouth, wash my pills down with grapefruit juice from the carton. I leave the cup in the sink, sorry Amy, no time, pull my rain poncho off the coat rack, stuff my wallet and keys into my pants pocket, and make my way down the two flights of stairs.

The hallway smells like chili and cabbage, and the walls look like they've been painted to match, brownish-red below the molding and a kind of pale off-green above. The place hasn't been repainted in years, and parts have flaked off to show a coat of mustard yellow underneath.

I don't mind it, though, because once you get upstairs, it makes our place look that much nicer. At the end of the downstairs hallway twelve mailboxes are lined up, a little crooked because the floor has buckled over time. They remind me of hollow tin soldiers, patiently waiting to have their contents removed and inspected. I know that there isn't going to be anything in our box, but like a fool I take out my keys and open it to make sure. I'm right. Or wrong, depending. Nothing there. It's not even going to be in the mailbox anyhow. It's a package, not a letter, and when it comes, if it ever does, I'll probably find it on the floor along with the other UPS and FedEx deliveries that they casually toss into the hall.

Maybe I should call and find out when it's going to arrive, just an estimate, really, that's all I need. Then I can be on the lookout for it. Maybe even take a day off so I can be home when it comes. I can take a personal day. I used up all my sick leave and vacation time for the operation, and the museum gave me an extra week of unpaid leave too. But maybe I can coax just one more day out of them. Get someone to cover my shift.

Time to get going. I shut the door to the building behind me and step out into the street. It's not even close to rush hour but it's already sticky and humid, low rain clouds fat with moisture, and it's going to get a lot worse. I turn left toward the subway, careful about how I walk. It's two long blocks, good practice. I pull my shoulders up, take a wide stride, and rock my hips, loose and easy, planting each foot firmly in front of the other. I swing my arms at my sides, and look straight ahead, frowning slightly. Don't mess with me. Don't even come close.

I'm always the first to arrive. I hang my poncho in the guard's closet under the stairs, then punch in and unlock the glass security station. I pull the big ring of master keys from the desk and head upstairs, where I open the electrical box to turn on the gallery lights. On my way to unlock the gate that covers the front doors, I pass my favorite piece, a sculpture that's on loan to the museum. After I open up, I'll stop to look at it for a minute. The gate is heavy, and pulling it to one side makes me feel as though the muscles of my chest wall are going to rip. I try to use the strength in my shoulders and back instead.

Walking through the cool galleries, I stop and lean over to look at the sculpture, which I do every chance I get. It's the most realistic figure I've ever seen, a naked man lying on his back on a low white platform. His eyes are closed, his arms at his sides, palms up, his feet turned out. He looks so peaceful, like he's sleeping. Only he's not sleeping, he's dead. You can tell by the waxy, greenish color of his skin, the pink bruising around his eyes, the way his body has let go of its own weight. He has dark hair and stubble on his chin, and his eyelashes are long, almost like a girl's. His pale arms and legs are covered with sparse, dark hairs.

His dick has fallen to one side, surrounded by a wiry thicket, like Brillo. The word that comes to my mind is woebegone. If you get really close, you can make out the bluish veins running along its shaft. He's circumcised, and you can see the little slit at the end, just exactly right. You'd swear his penis was made of flesh. The testicles look soft and puckery, and make me think that if I touched them they'd feel like stewed prunes, even though I know they're made of silicone. I'm fascinated by this part of him. I feel as if I stare at it long enough, absorb very detail of it, I'll be able to understand what he was like, how he felt about things, who he loved. The whole figure looks absolutely real, trust me, but everyone can tell it isn't, because it's only about three feet long. It's called *Dead Dad*, by an Australian artist named Ron Mueck, and the label says that it's a portrait of the artist's father.

I always feel like covering him up or something, even when there's no one looking at him. When the museum is open, I see people congregated around the platform, absolutely silent, some kneeling down to get a closer look, others just standing with their heads bowed. I wonder if Mueck's father actually died, or if he just made the sculpture by trying to imagine what he'd look like dead. And if he's alive, I wonder if his dad minded, or if he took it as a compliment. I'd guess the latter, because it's such a loving portrait, even if he's dead. Or maybe because of it.

The Museum doesn't open till 11:00, but the staff is going to be trailing in any minute now, so I can't dawdle. I like to have everything in shape before Simpson arrives. He's my supervisor, and he's got a sharp eye, especially when it comes to me. I've been at the museum for six years, but when I came back to work after the operation, I wasn't sure how he felt about me anymore. More than once I've caught him staring at me, looking like he had an important question he wanted to ask. Simpson's not bad, but he's got a chip on his shoulder the size of a baseball plate. Probably got it from watching his own back, since he's the only supervisor in the whole place who isn't white.

This morning, though, he seems subdued. "Hi, there," he says, glancing briefly at a spot above my head. He never calls me by my first name anymore, but then, hardly anyone does. My co-workers always find a way around it.

"So, how's it going, kid?" Tomiko asks.

"Whatcha up to, Slim?" Sherelle wants to know.

"Hey, I'd like you to meet my brother Greg," Barton says, not introducing me by name to the burly guy at his side. I'm used to it, or almost. Nancy, up in payroll, still calls me Clara, but I'm always surprised when she does. And she's way too nice to me, asking how I'm feeling, making some comment or other about how much better I'm looking these days, how my hair is getting longer, isn't it nice to see me putting on a little weight.

The other security guards trickle in, all within ten minutes of each other. I say good morning to each of them, point to the white board where I've used the erasable marker to scrawl their assignments for the day, and then sit down to adjust the surveillance monitors.

I'm overqualified for the job, but I don't care. I chose it because I don't have to take my work home with me, and because I love museums, always have. Even more important, I'm a city employee, so matter what, they're not going to fire me. Matter of fact, they can't, because we're contracted by the city and the union covers us. So I'm not about to go looking for anything else. Besides, I'm always going to be overqualified, unless the job market for amateur poets with degrees in sociology suddenly opens up.

At 4:00, I punch out. The museum doesn't close till eight tonight, and someone else is scheduled to lock up. If I move fast, I'll be early enough to miss the subway rush, maybe even get home in time to sign for the package if I have to.

By the time I climb out of the subway the heat is stifling and the straps have begun to chafe. There'll be welts for sure, maybe even a blister or two. I'm tired of it, tired of sprinkling talcum under the elastic, tired of feeling the powder clump up into irritating, grainy little nodules. Tired of the whole fucking thing. The hole fucking thing. Not feeling whole.

I take the front stairs two at a time, opening the outer door so hard it bangs, and race into the hallway. The packages, as usual, are piled carelessly under the stairs, and I paw through them, looking for my name. Nothing. I stick the key in the mailbox, pull out a handful of bills, a crumpled supermarket flyer, and the *New Yorker*. I bend down to make sure there's nothing shoved in there where I can't see it right off. Sure enough, crammed way in the back of the narrow space is a cardboard box.

TP/Inc.'s discrete logo, placed above the return address, doesn't give a clue as to what's in the package. Tucking it under my arm, I climb the two worn wooden flights of stairs and use my hip to lodge the box against the doorframe while I open the top, then the bottom lock of our door. It's cool and dark inside. Amy won't be home for a couple of hours, which is a relief. She's left the air conditioner on for a change, and I'm grateful. I scoot the package back up under my arm and close the door behind me.

At the table, I slit the clear tape that holds the top edges of the box together, cutting the address label in half. The top flap, "C. Breslow," lifts up, separating me from my apartment, my street, my city. Inside, layers of bubble wrap are scotch-taped around a plastic sleeve, inside which is the item that I've paid over $900 for, covered in layers of white tissue paper. I open the tissue slowly, sheet by sheet, making love to it.

It lies there, pink and ivory, with faint traces of brown in exactly the right places. Smaller than I'd imagined, but more realistic, too. It's soft against my index finger, smooth, resilient, just like the real thing. Or what I think the real thing feels like. I'm staring down at it, trying to imagine what it's going to look like once it's in place when I hear the key turn in the lock. Shit. She's early.

I cram everything back in the box and grab my poncho from the floor where I dropped it, folding it over the package. When the door opens, I smile cheerfully at Amy, whose arms are full of groceries, a bouquet of red and orange flowers lodged under one arm.

"Let me put my coat away and I'll give you a hand," I say, turning to the bedroom. I shove the box to the back of my side of the closet, behind my hiking boots, and rush back out to take the groceries out of Amy's arms.

"Yum," I say, "you've been to the farmer's market."

Amy plops into a chair. She's five foot two, a curvy ball of energy, dark hair standing straight out from her head in a wiry tangle, as though she's plugged into a socket. Brown eyes, bright and slightly unfocused behind red granny glasses. Coffee ice cream skin. Clothes that look like they've been plucked from a Goodwill bin, only there are fancy labels sewed into the seams.

"I finished the Ghost Girl project, so I called it a day," she says, "but I couldn't face the supermarket. Too crowded. So I stopped at Union Square instead. Supper will be ready by 8:00—*if* that's okay with you." She sounds irritated.

I look over at her. We always eat at the same time, at least when we're home, and Amy never asks. Did I do something to annoy her, or was it something that happened at work?

"What's up, sweetie?" I ask. "Did you have a bad day?"

Amy works at a company that designs computer games for teenage girls, and there's so much that can go wrong that Amy comes home frustrated and pissed off a lot of the time.

"No," says Amy. "But we have to talk."

Uh-oh, here it is. I knew it was coming, but I didn't think it would be so soon.

When we first met, I felt this little chill go up my back and the hair on my arms stood straight up. It was at an all-girl dinner for our friend Shariza, who was having her first big show, and the minute I saw Amy, I knew I'd try to get her to come home with me that night.

I liked her wide smile, the gap in her front teeth, her delicate hands. And the way she moved, as though no one were watching her. I thought she was the least self-conscious person I'd ever seen, outside of those subway crazies who are locked away in their own warped worlds. Amy was hardly crazy. She turned out to be smart, super-smart, but she didn't act like she knew it, or like anyone else was supposed to, either.

I didn't think Amy was my type at first, at least not for anything long-term. For one thing, she'd been married. It lasted less than a year, and even though they got along, she broke up with him because, she said, she couldn't stand waking up every morning with his thing poking her in the behind. But she hadn't had a lot of experience with women, so I was afraid that she might change her mind. It had happened to me before. The other thing was, she was a computer geek. When she wasn't sitting in front of the big fancy screens at work, you could usually find her in a corner with her head in her laptop. But to my surprise, she liked poetry, too.

In her spare time, Amy loved to fix things. A frozen window, a leak under the sink, a lamp that needed rewiring. She could program the VCR, repair the stereo, reinstall a hard drive. For someone so small, she was surprisingly strong, hauling stuff in from the street to patch, refinish, rebuild. And she was a terrific cook, too.

I was the opposite. Couldn't boil an egg. If something broke, I threw it out. What I liked was sports. When I was young I was a sprinter, even tried my hand at hurdles. I played basketball, volleyball, handball. In the winter, I did speed skating. Once I was out of school, I gave up competitive sports, but I was a sucker for white-water rafting, skiing, rock climbing. It didn't go with being a poet, but then, hardly anything did. I wrote my poetry late at night, usually in bed, propped up on my elbows with a mechanical pencil and a little thin-lined Japanese notebook. Once in a while, I'd get something published in *Grand Street* or *Poet's Corner*, and twice I'd gone to an artist's colony in Vermont, where I could write most of the day and then hike and climb when I finished working. Amy wasn't interested. Her idea of a vacation was to go to the Ars Electronica conference in Linz, Austria and butt heads with other computer nerds. I didn't mind, because there was great skiing around there.

We've been a couple for almost five years. Within the first year of being together, we found a great apartment on the Upper West Side. It had a decent workroom for Amy and a little study off the bedroom for me. The kitchen was big, the bathroom was small, and there was a modest living room with two high windows facing the street. Between the two of us, it was affordable, and it came with a five-year lease, renewable. For New York, it was a prize. We'd been there ever since.

We had friends, money, a life.

I'd always been a tomboy, nothing wrong with that. I had lots of girlfriends I hung out with, but boys didn't interest me, and even though my mother told me that I'd grow out of it, I never did. They were no great mystery to me. I never dated a boy, never kissed one, never slept with one. It's no loss as far as I'm concerned.

Amy and I were happy. Sex started out great and stayed that way. I'm crazy about her smell, her body temperature, the way her little breasts point straight out, even when she's lying down. She has the best belly button in the whole world. I think she's beautiful, even if she doesn't think so herself. Well, who does, really? I'd just as soon never look in a mirror again, even though Amy is always telling me that she likes the way I move, how I dress, my high cheekbones and my large nose, which she calls "distinguished." She says I'm elegant, but that's the last thing in the world I want to be.

About a year ago, before it all started, we were visiting Sue and Marian, who have a summer place in the Catskills, and we'd gone on a hike, just a short one, because Amy gets irritated when bugs fly around her head. She was worried about poison ivy, too. The four of us were tromping down this wide path in the woods, birds twittering, sun filtering through the tall trees, a breeze blowing. A perfect day, really. I gave her arm a squeeze and yelled ahead to the other two to wait up for me, I had to pee. I stepped off the path into the bushes, pulled down my hiking shorts and squatted. It suddenly struck me that it was wrong: I was supposed to be standing, peeing out in a wide arc that landed at the base of the oak tree over there. I shouldn't be doing this, didn't want to be doing this. I wasn't a girl, for Chrissake, and I was not going to goddamn behave like one. I could feel my face go red and the air go out of me like I was choking.

The thing is, though, I was. A woman, that is. I had all the equipment, big breasts even, and although I'd always been a tomboy, I was still a girl tomboy. Nobody ever mistook me for a boy when I was a kid, or a teenager, or when I hit thirty-five, for that matter. What is it they politely call us? "Women-identified women." I was a lesbian, and happy to be one. But you couldn't necessarily tell just by looking at me. Of course, you rarely can tell what someone is just by looking at them.

Surprisingly, my mother was okay with it, even early on. When she divorced my dad, she used to say that her hetero days were over, that if only she were younger, she'd take up with another woman. But she never did. Relationships were more trouble than they were worth, she said.

So I put the groceries away, and sit down across from Amy, my hands flat on the table. I stare at my knuckles, at the bones that stick out the sides of my wrists. What does she want to talk about now that she couldn't talk about yesterday, or the day before, or last week?

"What do you want to talk about?" I ask out loud.

"What's happening to us," she says, clearing her throat. "What's happening to you."

"Look," I say, "I've told you, I can't explain it. I felt like I'd been cheating, lying to myself all along, trying to pretend that I was something I wasn't. I mean, I was, but I wasn't. I'm the same person who loves you now as I was when I met you, it's just that I can see myself more clearly. The outside was all wrong, and that's the only thing that's changing. Once I fix it, I'll feel better. I won't be so tense." I look over at her to see if she gets it. She has a scowl on her face. "Besides," I continue, "it's the medication. It's making me nuts. I can't tell what kind of mood I'm in until it's too late to do anything about it."

"But how can you say you're the same," she asks, "when you're different? You don't look the same. I don't even recognize your voice on the telephone. Your walk has changed. You don't have boobs any more." Her voice has turned into a wail, and the end of her nose is red.

"Okay," I say, "but I didn't exactly have a choice about that. I know you think I did, but you were there, you heard what they told me. If I wanted to make absolutely sure, they said, I should have them both removed. Lofton is a good doctor, she wouldn't have suggested it as an option if she didn't want me to take it seriously." She doesn't respond.

"Amy," I ask gently, "what do you want me to do, here?"

"I know," she mutters, "but it was more than that. You didn't have to take it that far. You didn't have to become something you're not." She turns her head away and stares out the kitchen window.

I know what she's talking about, it's not that I don't. But cancer's funny.

Sometimes it isn't just the horror most people think it is. It can be a chance for something else to happen, something good. Hard to explain to anyone else, though. Even Amy.

When I first got diagnosed, she went into action. All those websites, list serves, support groups. Every night I'd go to bed alone, seeing her silhouette through the doorway of her room, the glow of the computer screen reflected in her glasses. Information overload. She had it all worked out, planned, signed, sealed, addressed, stamped, delivered, return receipt requested. Everything from TRAM flap surgery to silicone implants to nipple tattooing, all the news, all the time. "Look," she said, "you don't have to have the other one removed. Here are the percentages." She waved sheets of figures at me every morning, every night. Diagrams, before-and-after JPEGs, testimonials, links to alternative and complementary medicine, yoga, meditation, journaling retreats for women with cancer.

What I was thinking all along is, okay, why not go the whole way and find out what it's like? Other people pay huge amounts of money to have it done when they're perfectly healthy, and everyone is horrified. In my case, all I'll get is support. Pity, too, but I suppose it comes with the territory.

I wasn't even afraid, not after talking to Lofton. She was going to do the surgery herself. She'd been at it a long time. I had the feeling she liked me, that she'd do a good job. That I wasn't just another statistic to her. Maybe it was because I told her I was a poet, who knows? I also asked her to help me think through the "after" part, whether I'd need more surgery or hormones, and what kind.

So Amy knows all this. But she's still upset. I'm talking to her back. "Please come sit down," I plead. "You were the one who wanted to discuss it in the first place."

She turns around slowly, comes over and sits down. "Okay, you want to know, I'll tell you how I feel. I feel like you betrayed me. I feel like you threw our life together out the window. I could handle all the months of chemo when you stopped eating and going out and even talking to me. I could handle the doctors' visits and tests and even your being angry all the time." She looks away. "But I can't cope with not knowing who you are anymore."

I don't know how to answer. I don't feel like I've changed that much, even if I do look different. I looked even more different when I lost all my hair, but that didn't seem to throw her as much as this does. I know she's been through a lot, dealing with me, but I didn't get sick on purpose, and we agreed that we'd see each other through, no matter what. Five years is nothing to sneeze at, even without the legal papers.

"I love you, Amy," I say, "and that hasn't changed. I'm still me. Maybe even more me than I was before." Is she going to leave me? Is it that bad? I'd heard there were some good shrinks who specialized in this kind of thing.

"What if we went to counseling?" I ask her. "Would that help? I'll do anything you want, but I can't go back to what I was, not physically and not mentally, either." I take a deep breath. "Do you want to break up, is that it?"

Amy looks sad and uncertain. Her hands are clasped and she's squeezing her fingers together till they look like red and white worms. I have that queasy feeling in my stomach, the one that ping-pongs back into my chest and squeezes into a hard little ball of fear just behind my breastbone. I look straight into her eyes, waiting.

"No," she says, looking back at me. "I don't want to break up. It's just that I can't see a way out."

"Let's leave it for tonight," I suggest. "Let's make a nice dinner, have a glass of wine, put a little music on, dance. I'll be your sous-chef. Just tell me what to do." I move my chair closer to hers. "Please, Amy? Just for tonight? Let's be happy, please?"

The garlic and rosemary chicken is great, the roast potatoes perfect, the string beans crisp and bright green. I've torn the salad greens into bite-sized bits with extra care, put in sliced radishes and scallions, even toasted some pecans and added them at the last minute. We manage to talk about other things, like her newest project, an Amazonian web adventure game in which girls get to save each other from all the dangerous, exotic creatures in the jungle without killing them. She's thinking of having the animals taken to a wildlife refuge, with points for the number of creatures that survive and procreate.

By the time we finish dinner and I wash the dishes, the atmosphere seems to have calmed down. We get ready for bed, and for once she joins me, reaching for her book as I take my notebook and pencil from the night table drawer. I look over. She's reading *Dog Eaters*, a novel about the Philippines. I guess she's thinking about her family back there, still trying to come to terms with why it's been more than three years since they last came to visit her. I don't want to remind her that it might not be the United States that's the problem, but the fact that she's living with me.

We turn the lights off after a little while, and I move toward her in the dark, putting my arms around her back, fitting my hips against her warm butt, kissing her on the neck.

"Goodnight, honey," I murmur. "Don't worry, we'll figure it out."

She sighs, coughs, and snuggles closer. For the moment, I'm convinced we will.

After a few minutes, Amy's breathing becomes slow and regular. I wait a while, just to be sure. When enough time has passed and even my nudging her hard doesn't get a response, I pull away, swing my legs over the side of the bed, and carefully ease my feet into my slippers. I make my way over to the closet, sliding the door open slowly, praying that it doesn't squeak. It's like I've got night goggles on or something, I find the package so fast. I lift it out over my shoes, shut the closet door as slowly as I opened it, and move like a ghost out through the kitchen into the living room.

First, I read the instructions. It comes with medical adhesive, super-glue for the skin. And it's practical, because it also has a clear plastic tube with a kind of hollow suction-cup looking thing at one end. It's completely hidden, which makes everything realistic enough that no one is going to throw me out of the john. And washable, of course. The most amazing thing is that it can be used for sex, too, by holding it a certain way. Or so the instructions say.

I take it into the bathroom and lock the door, then climb onto the sink and kneel, one knee on either side of the basin, so I can check it out. This mirror assumes that everything you have to do in the bathroom is going to be from the shoulders up, but our only full-length one is in the bedroom, and no way am I going to risk that.

Now, I'm pure torso. I look like one of those Greek statues with all its appendages missing. I thought about what it must be like to be the statue when it was about to have some meticulously reconstructed vital part—an arm, a foot, a breast—permanently, seamlessly, reattached. Then I see myself lying down, like Dead Dad, and wonder what it would be like. Would I wish that I were still alive? Would I worry about how I looked to all those people? I remind myself that sculptures don't think, don't feel, don't want.

Even though I have the thing in hand, so to speak, I'm not planning to use it right away. First of all, I need to practice, and then I have to figure out how to break it to Amy. There's a good chance that she'll totally freak out, so I have to go easy, let her get used to the idea before I actually try it out on her.

She knows I've been stuffing things down there. First a pair of balled up socks, but they kept moving around. Then I tried making one, with condoms and hair gel. That was better, but still uncomfortable. Then I found a ready-made, which is what I've been using, but it needs a harness to hold it in place and the damned thing itches and rubs. I think I may be allergic to the elastic or something. Amy glares at me when she sees me putting it on, so I try not to do it when she's around, and I usually take it off first thing when I get home, so she doesn't get on my case.

"Why do you have to wear that stupid thing?" she says. "Do you think it fools anybody? Do you think it's attractive, your stupid strap-on? It's not even the same color as your skin. It makes you look like a clown."

That kind of comment is just not helpful. Even if she thinks so, she could keep it to herself. No matter how much I try to explain, she doesn't understand. She says that I'm in denial about who I am, that I have old issues that haven't been resolved. Whenever I hear that, I think tissues, old tissues that haven't been dissolved. She refuses to call me Cody, although I beg her to, try to explain that I need to move away from Clara toward something else. I even filed the papers to change my name legally, but she says fuck Cody. She doesn't want any part of him. She wants Clara and won't settle for anything less. Or rather, more.

And then she complains that cancer was what did it, that the stress and chemo and meds messed with my head and made me decide to become something I'm not. But I know that all it did was open the door and let in some light.

The museum is quiet today. It's Monday, and we're closed to the public, so it's when we catch up on all the stuff we can't do when people are wandering around looking at the exhibits. I like Mondays because they're slow, and because I get to spend more time looking at the art instead of being mostly stuck downstairs, glued to the monitors. After I open, I decide to check on my little guy, see how he's doing. I also want to take a closer look at his parts, now that I have something to compare them to. Or maybe it's the other way around, that I want to see how mine compare to his. Not size-wise, because his are tiny, relatively speaking. Not in relation to his body, of course. They're pretty much okay there, not too small, not too big. Mine comes in three-and-a-half inch, five-inch and seven-inch sizes, custom-blended to your skin tone, and you know which one I got. I'm not a shrinking violet, but I'm not one to parade my wares, either. Like Goldilocks, the one I ordered was just right.

I squat down and stare at *Dead Dad*'s groin. Did the artist ask his father to pose? How did he know what his dick looked like? Did he just make it up, or try to remember from the last time he'd seen it, when he was a kid, maybe? Or perhaps his dad wasn't shy, walked around the house naked sometimes, when Mueck could have gotten a good look at it. Maybe Mueck just used his own as a model. Dad's looks pretty specific. It's not the kind of generic thing you find with the cheaper Packers, where they all look exactly alike except they come in "light" or "dark."

So it's no use comparing, only I can't help it. It occurs to me that I'm acting just like a guy, sizing the others up, seeing how I stack up. Then I think about Amy's ex-husband. I wonder what his looked like. I never asked her, but now's probably not the time to start.

Amy calls me from work, tells me she's going to be home late. The Amazon animal rescue and rehab deal didn't fly with the client. Too goody-goody. She's got to go back to the drawing board, no metaphor intended. She suggests we get take-out, around nine. I tell her it's okay, no problem, see you then, hope the project works out, and when I hang up I realize that I can't wait to get home. It's only three, but I still have a lot of work to do to get ready for tomorrow's security walk-through, because a new show is opening that night. People know how to behave at the Met or the Frick, but when it comes to contemporary art, there's no telling how they're going to respond. Sometimes people even get into arguments with the work, yelling at pieces they don't like. Can you imagine? But it's a lot more interesting than guarding all those statues and precious objects in the old museums, where hardly anything out of the ordinary ever happens.

I finish in plenty of time, straighten up my desk, wipe down the assignment board, and go upstairs to chat with Barton. He's one of the ones who doesn't seem to even notice what's happening to me. He's originally from Wisconsin, so maybe people back there are just more relaxed than the rest of us. Post-op, he was happy to see me again, no questions asked. Barton's easy to be around, but only for short periods of time, because he's always at the same emotional pitch, always friendly and wise-cracking, but never talking about anything real. He treats every personal comment, about himself or anyone else, as though it was a subpoena.

Today's no different. "Hey, what's shakin,' pal," he says when he sees me. "Howdja like the weather out there? Gonna rain for sure, maybe any minute now.

Yesterday was okay, a little humid, but today's a real pisser." I nod seriously, trying to convey the impression that after thoughtful consideration, I completely agree. He's pleased. Then leans forward, whispers conspiratorially, "So, did I tell ya about my cousin Cindy? She was engaged to a guy with a wooden leg, but broke it off." He explodes into raucous laughter, slapping me on the back. I laugh too, punch him lightly in the upper arm, and say goodnight. "Watch out for runaway puns," I tell him, "it's dangerous out there."

By the time I get home, I've got a headache. I go straight to the medicine cabinet, take three Advils, then get undressed, peeling off the old harness and pack and tossing the contraption on the floor of the closet. I jump into the shower, and by the time I'm done, I feel better. Maybe tonight will be the night. Why not try it out right away? There's no reason to wait.

Amy comes home at quarter to nine, sweaty and tired, and I'm glad that I've already ordered. Thai, her favorite kind, from the more expensive restaurant, the one that has better food. I have a bottle of white wine chilling in the fridge, and a Schubert sonata playing in the background. I'm dressed in a white linen shirt, Levi's 501s, and I'm wearing the thick silver link chain she gave me for my thirty-fifth birthday. She likes the way it looks against my skin, she says, and although any jewelry at all other than my watch makes me feel strange, I do it to please her. Which I'm trying hard to do right now.

I love the way she bursts through the door, always with her arms full, even if it's just stuff from the office that she's crammed into a paper sack at the last minute. I thought people who worked in technology wouldn't need anything more than a small satchel for their CDs, or maybe not even that, maybe just a USB portable drive on their keychain, but it seems that they produce more paper than anyone, except maybe lawyers. This time, she's also got a CVS bag with shampoo, three kinds of cold remedies, Slim-Fast bars, and some Day-Glo gift wrap. Plus a Barnes & Noble bag half full of new books. She obviously went shopping on her lunch break, something she thinks of as relaxing. Me, I'd rather drag a two-hundred-pound boulder up a hill than go shopping. But between us, I guess you'd say it all works out. Or did.

I take some of the packages out of her arms and give her a kiss on the cheek. "More client problems?" I ask, hoping to hell there weren't, not today.

"Not really," she says. "I fixed up the project by making the town they're based in have a coup d'etat. That way the girls have their hands full dealing with armed rebels and trying to create a coalition government. Points for every person they can convince to vote, or something like that. Haven't figured it out, but I will." She gives me a resigned look. "I don't suppose you've done anything about dinner," she says, looking around the kitchen, mouth pursed.

"It's on its way. Taste of Thailand, in five minutes. Let me pour you a glass of wine."

When the food arrives, she comes back into the kitchen. She's changed into drawstring pants and a tank top, pulled her hair into an unruly top knot, and washed off her makeup. Her face looks cool and creamy. She has on the little diamond studs her grandmother gave her, and they twinkle in her ears when she moves her head. The odors coming from the containers on the counter are tantalizing, and my mouth waters. I'm hungry, but I can't imagine eating because my stomach has decided to enter the Olympic 400-meter hurdles, going for the gold.

I don't know how to begin this time, how to get her used to the idea without scaring her away altogether. My new equipment is nestled comfortably in my jeans, ready and willing to do its work. Me, too. I'm ready and willing. It's been a while since we've made love like we used to, when our coming together was a deep conversation, a connection that left us both feeling peaceful and secure. Knowing we belonged to each other, that nothing could ever come between us.

I am so tired. Right now, I want this more than anything in the world. For the first time since the operation, I feel like I'm on my way home. It's such a relief I literally don't know what to do with myself. I tell myself that Amy will come around because she loves me. Because we have a history together. Because I need her to.

I empty the food from the containers into bowls and platters, set out the cloth napkins and serving spoons, the silver and enamel chopsticks we gave each other for our first anniversary, pour ice water into the big pale green glasses we save for special occasions. As I reach up to the top shelf to get the wine cooler down, I hear her hand slap the table, hard. I look around, and she's staring at me with a strange expression. Not at me, exactly, at my crotch.

"What's going on, here?" she asks angrily. "Why are you wearing that thing again? And why does it look different? Did you make it bigger?"

I come back to the table. This is going to be harder than I thought. "Look, Amy, let's eat first, and then we can talk."

"No," she says, "I don't feel like it. I want to know what the hell is going on. You think eating is going to make it go away, but it's not going away. I want Clara back, for Chrissake! And that stupid roll of socks isn't helping."

"It's not socks," I tell her. "It's the real thing, or at least the closest to it I can get. I want you to at least give it—give me—a chance."

Okay, the hell with the food. I stand up, lean over and pick her up out of the chair, scooping her up in my arms like a bride. She's so surprised that nothing comes out of her mouth, which is frozen into a big O. I carry her to the bedroom, kick the door closed behind me, and gently deposit her on the bed, nuzzling her neck the whole time. She pushes at me half-heartedly, while I whisper, "Come on, Amy, just this once, give it a try." She shuts her eyes tight, lets me take off her clothes while I kiss her ears, her mouth, her wrists. I take my own shirt off, harder because I don't want to take the time to unbutton it and I have to pull it over my head instead, which hurts so bad I almost cry out, but then it's done and I can lower my arms and undo my jeans, pushing them off and shoving them over the end of the bed.

I roll over to Amy, covering the top half of her body with the top half of mine, feeling the warmth of her skin, loving its softness, its resilience, smelling her familiar sweet scent. After a while, when her body relaxes and opens, I ease one leg slowly over hers. I reach down and take my new penis in my hand, maneuver it out and up, and let my whole torso rest on hers. Then I move quickly, and it's inside her before she knows what's happened.

Amy lets out a shriek. There isn't much of a warm-up, so of course she's surprised, but I thought she might enjoy it, once she got used to it. She was never much for the dildo routine, because she said it struck her as aggressive. I'm the opposite. I like it because it makes me feel powerful. Still, sex is always a compromise, and I don't mind toning it down for Amy, who always said that she was drawn to women because we *are* different—in bed, too. She never liked "imitation" anything, in the kitchen or the bedroom.

What I don't expect is her reaction. She turns over, pushing me off, staring down at my new add-on, and slaps it, hard. The blow pulls the skin under it so violently it makes me bite my tongue, but it doesn't detach. The glue is as strong as they said it was. The force of her hand, though, has whacked it into its down position.

Her face is creased into a fist of rage. "You stupid asshole," she snarls, "I've had it with you. Is that what you wanted, to fuck me? Well, you've done it. Are you happy now?"

I'm staring at the food congealing in the plates, the Pad Thai noodles lying sodden under a faint sheen of grease, the pale summer rolls lined up like fat, limp dicks. Amy's gone. The clothes that she didn't take are crumpled on the floor of the closet. Her dresser drawers are open, underwear and nightgowns and socks half in, half out. She took her toothbrush, her deodorant, her shampoo. The last thing she grabbed on her way out was the coffee pot.

"You don't get it," she screamed at me over her shoulder. "I want to be with a woman, not a man!" She slammed the door so hard I felt the floor shake.

Funny how quiet it can get, even in the city, even this early at night. No sirens, no car alarms, no dogs barking. I think I can hear my heart beating, though.

I get up slowly, my legs a little unsteady. I walk over to the bedroom mirror and stare at myself. My hair sticks out like Dagwood's, and my mouth is narrowed into a thin line. I've lost some weight since the operation, and my hands and feet look big and red. I take off the chain around my neck and put it in the empty water glass by my side of the bed. The blue T-shirt I threw on comes to the middle of my thighs, and I reach underneath and change things to the erect position, so the shirt pulls up in front. Then I take it off and have a good hard look. In the dim light, you can't tell that it's not real. You can hardly see the scars on my chest, either.

I clear my throat. "Cody," I say. "Hey, Cody," a little louder. "What's shaking?" I plant my feet shoulder-width apart and cross my arms over my chest. Isn't that what guys do all the time, love 'em and leave 'em? Might as well get used to it. Of course, it was the other way around this time. Amy left me. Or was it really me who left her first?

All of a sudden it occurs to me that Dead Dad was too young to die. That's why all the people gathered around his body look so sad. I feel sorry for him too, for everything he missed, for the others in his family who are missing him. There must be plenty of men in the world who are decent, who have friends and feelings. And they aren't all gay, either. This one must have been a good husband, a loving father. He and his son were probably close, did lots of stuff together, talked about things that mattered. A tragedy, really.

My throat tightens and the tears well up, but then I start thinking, how many women do you suppose he fucked before he met Mueck's mother? Was he faithful to her after they got married? I wonder if he ever walked out on someone he loved. Or maybe it's the other way around, that he was there for them all along, caring, considerate, fun to be around.

I tell myself that I'll go by and take another look at him tomorrow.

BIOGRAPHY

Marcia Tucker (1940–2006) was founder and director (1977–99) of the New Museum of Contemporary Art, a museum located in New York City dedicated to innovative art and artistic practice. Her motto, "Act first, think later—that way you'll have something to think about," was a guiding principle in running the institution, which was during her tenure at the vanguard of the contemporary art world. She organized such major exhibitions as "The Time of Our Lives" (1999), "A Labor of Love" (1996), and "Bad Girls" (1994). She was the series editor of *Documentary Sources in Contemporary Art*, five books of theory and criticism co-published by the New Museum and The MIT Press. After resigning her director's post in 1999, she continued to write, and teach and lecture around the country.

Ms. Tucker was Curator of Painting and Sculpture at the Whitney Museum of American Art from 1969 to 1977, where she organized major exhibitions of the work of Bruce Nauman, Lee Krasner, Joan Mitchell, and Richard Tuttle, among others. She was the 1999 recipient of the Bard College Award for Curatorial Achievement, and received the Art Table Award for Distinguished Service to the Visual Arts in 2000.

THE ACADIA SUMMER ARTS PROGRAM

The Acadia Summer Arts Program—commonly referred to as A.S.A.P., Kippy's Kamp, and Kamp Kippy—is an internationally known summer artist residency, located in the breathtaking Acadia National Park on Mount Desert Island, Maine. Since 1993, the program has furnished invitees with the time, space, and resources to rejuvenate their creative practices. Each year, A.S.A.P. convenes an impressive array of artists and arts professionals including museum directors, curators, architects, painters, sculptors, filmmakers, musicians, poets, dancers, and historians. The island is dotted with A.S.A.P.'s private cottages, which guests are free to use as either peaceful work space or for simple rest and relaxation. Most of the guests' time is unstructured, but the program provides weekly communal activities—dinners, guest lectures, and boat excursions to the surrounding islands—and annual public events—exhibitions, film screenings, dance performances, and concerts.

Marion "Kippy" Boulton Stroud, A.S.A.P.'s founder, has had a lifelong passion for supporting and facilitating artistic production. In 1977, she founded the Fabric Workshop and Museum in Philadelphia, where she currently serves as Artistic Director. Having spent summers on Mount Desert Island since childhood, Kippy wanted to share the beautiful Maine landscape with her friends and colleagues. Beginning as a small gathering in Kippy's coastal home, Shore Cottage, the program has blossomed into a summer-long influx of over three hundred guests each year. Consequently, the physical space has evevolved into a complex of studios, offices, and lecture facilities designed by the late Steve Izenour of Venturi, Scott Brown and Associates. Despite this growth, the intimate, familial quality of A.S.A.P. remains intact.